3/01

J-B

Hodges, Margaret.
    The true tale of
Johnny Appleseed.

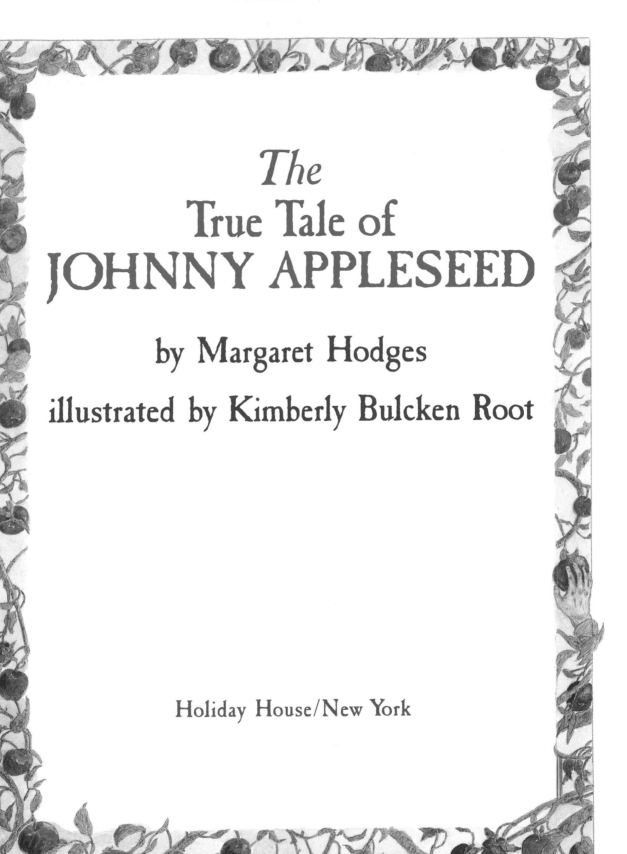

The
True Tale of
JOHNNY APPLESEED

by Margaret Hodges

illustrated by Kimberly Bulcken Root

Holiday House/New York

To Apple Street
M.H.

To the Lisse family
K.B.R.

J-B
CHAPMAN

Library of Congress Cataloging-in-Publication Data
Hodges, Margaret, 1911–
The true tale of Johnny Appleseed / by Margaret Hodges;
illustrated by Kimberly Bulcken Root. — 1st ed.
p.   cm.
Summary: Relates the story of the man who traveled west planting
apple seeds to make the country a better place to live.
ISBN 0-8234-1282-2 (library)
1. Appleseed, Johnny, 1774 – 1845 — Juvenile literature.   2. Apple
growers — United States — Biography — Juvenile literature.   3. Frontier
and pioneer life — Middle West — Juvenile literature.   [1. Appleseed,
Johnny, 1774 – 1845.   2. Apple growers.   3. Frontier and pioneer
life.]   I. Root, Kimberly Bulcken, ill.   II. Title.
SB63.C46H63   1997   96-30939   CIP   AC
634'.11'092 — dc20
[B]

His mush pan slapped on his windy head,
His torn shirt flapping, his eyes alight...

FRANCES FROST. An American Ghost.
New York Herald Tribune,
August 21, 1943.

Johnny Chapman was born in Leominster, Massachusetts, in 1774. When he was a baby, his mother made him a little hammock and hung it on the bough of an apple tree. He could hear his mother singing as she helped his father harvest their crop of apples:

> Rock-a-bye, baby, in the treetop;
> When the wind blows, the cradle will rock...

The apple trees! Every spring the blossoms were like white clouds. Every autumn, as Johnny grew up, he helped his parents pick the ripe fruit—tart and sweet and juicy.

In Johnny's mind an idea grew and grew. When he was twenty-three years old, he said good-bye to home and family and started westward. Ahead was a wilderness, and Johnny's dream was to plant apple trees there. He carried with him only a stewpot, a hatchet, a flint and steel for making fire, a bag of cornmeal, and a sack of apple seeds. A Bible was buttoned under his coat.

Those who saw him said that he put his stewpot on his head for a hat. He gave away his clothes to anyone who needed a coat or trousers or shoes. Most of the time he wore no shoes. One man said that he saw Johnny breaking the ice in a creek with a bare foot.

All along his path he planted apple seeds. If he was invited to spend the night in a cabin, he would not take a bed, but slept on the floor. He would not eat until he was sure that the children in the family were full. He loved honey but would never take it from a bee tree until he saw that the bees had enough honey to keep themselves alive during the winter. A strange man indeed!

He found fewer and fewer little settlements as
he traveled westward, following creeks and rivers
by canoe most of the way.

He had to cross the wild Allegheny mountains on foot, and a furious winter snowstorm caught him by surprise. Up to his knees in snow, he wrapped his feet in pieces of cloth torn from his coat. Then he wove long, thin beech tree branches into snowshoes.

With straps made of bark, he fastened his snowshoes to his feet and loped along over the top of the deep snow.

As time went by, Johnny walked so long and so far that his feet grew almost as tough as an animal's paws. In other ways, too, he came to be like an animal. He could curl up to sleep under a bush or in the hollow of a tree. Once when he had planned to spend the night in a fallen tree, he found a mother bear already there, asleep with her cubs. Johnny backed out and moved on. "That bear family has more right to the tree than I do," he said.

He would not even hurt a fly if he could help it. One of his sayings was, "Each creature is only acting according to its nature."

Some people thought he was crazy. They laughed when they saw him coming with his ragged coat, his bare feet, and his stewpot hat on his head. But children loved him. He would bring them simple gifts—a bit of calico to make a doll's dress, or a skipping rope. The children would run to him shouting, "Here comes Johnny Appleseed! Johnny Appleseed!" It was the children who first gave him his famous name.

As he traveled west, or came back East to tend his young trees, Johnny brought news to the settlers. It might be good or bad news about the Indians. The Indians never harmed Johnny Appleseed. They saw that he was unlike other white men on the frontier. He was wise, and ready to help anyone in need. The Indians listened to him as he tried to understand and speak their language.

Johnny would give the settlers news from back East and tell about his own adventures and narrow escapes. Then he would pull a book out from under his coat. It might be a Bible, or a book of sermons and prayers. He read so well that everyone listened, old and young, whether or not they understood the words. "This is news fresh from Heaven," he said.

When Johnny Appleseed talked about Heaven, his eyes shone. He said that each person had a body while he lived on earth, but in Heaven each one would be a spirit and would never die. When he looked up into an apple tree or up to the stars at night, he could almost see the angels as they praised God because He had made all things good.

Often, Johnny would take a book apart and leave sections in cabins along his way, picking them up on his next visit. They were a traveling library in the wilderness. With money from the sale of apple trees, Johnny bought more books as the old ones wore out. He gave trees to people who were too poor to pay. But Johnny himself never seemed to feel poor.

Planting, always planting! Slowly he moved from Pennsylvania to Ohio, often paddling along streams that had never been heard of back East—the wide Allegheny, little Brokenstraw Creek, the Muskingum, the Maumee, Licking River, and Owl Creek. Now he was in what the maps called "Indian Land." Only a few roads and Indian trails connected the white man's villages. But settlers were coming—whole families traveling by covered wagon, many carrying bags of apple seeds to plant orchards. Johnny's idea was spreading.

As he went farther and farther on into the wilderness, he kept ahead of the newcomers. In five or six years, when they picked a place for a village, Johnny's apple trees were waiting for them and made the wilderness seem more like home.

In early March 1845, Johnny had got as far west as Fort Wayne, Indiana, and was staying with the family of an old friend when he heard that cattle had broken into one of his new orchards, fifteen miles away. The weather was cold and wet, but he set off at once and never stopped to rest on the long walk. "Cloudy. Snow showers," an Indiana farmer wrote in his diary that day.

The next day the weather report was, "Snow showers all day." When Johnny got back to his friends' house, they put him to bed with a high fever. During the March snows, Johnny Appleseed died, and his body returned to the earth he had loved. By early April, winter was past. The weather report read, "In the night thunder showers—then fair—first apple blossoms."

Johnny's work was done. He had made the wilderness bloom. Ever since, clouds of white apple blossoms have filled the Pennsylvania, Ohio, and Indiana river valleys, and in the fall, children growing up where there had been only wilderness have had apples, apple butter for their bread, applesauce, apple pies, and apple cider. All through the winter they can reach into a barrel and pull out an apple to munch. Oh, the beautiful apples!

Johnny's apple trees lived on and on. Orchard after orchard, they spread along the river valleys. Some say that every apple tree you see in the Middle West comes from a Johnny Appleseed tree.

Johnny himself was not forgotten. The children to whom he had told stories about his adventures passed the stories on to their own children.

The Indians remembered too. They said, "He was our Medicine Man."

And farm folks will tell you that when the apple trees make a cloud of white in the springtime, you may still catch a glimpse of something or someone moving among the branches at the far end of your orchard. It may be the spirit of Johnny Appleseed come down from Heaven to tend his trees.

AUTHOR'S NOTE

Johnny Appleseed in History

When America won its Revolutionary War against Great Britain, the new country, the United States, began to grow fast. It was a big country. President George Washington was offering land in the West at only a few dollars an acre.

This land was in western Ohio where there were few settlers. Beyond that, the maps said "Indian Land." Life in the West would be hard, but many young men wanted to try it, thinking that they could "get rich quick." Others were in trouble with the law and hoped to disappear into the wilderness. Some just liked to be on the move. Most men going west carried a rifle.

Once again, in 1812, war broke out between Great Britain and its old colonies in America. The British were joined by the Indians of Ohio, who saw that the settlers were encroaching on their territory. By sudden raid and ambush, by burning cabins and attacking many settlers, they tried to drive the invaders back to the Ohio River.

But settlers kept on coming west. They built strong blockhouses for protection, and they took their revenge. They burned Indian villages, killed Indian women and children as well as men, and deceived and cheated Indians who had trusted them.

Johnny was different. He was friendly to people of all sorts; he was an educated man and a great reader, a natural gentleman. He loved the outdoor life, and the frontier was calling him.

This is how he did his work. With his axe he would clear trees and brush from a few acres of good soil. He pushed apple seeds into the rich earth and piled up a brushwood fence around his plantings to protect them from rabbits and deer. When his sacks were empty, he headed back to civilization where there were orchards and cider mills to supply him with more seeds. Every year he came back to visit his new orchards and pick out some young trees that were ready to be moved. Then, by canoe, by settler's wagon, or on horseback, when he could borrow or buy an old horse, he headed back to the wilderness!

During Johnny's lifetime, few people had ever heard of Johnny Chapman. But in time to come, his country knew him well by his other name, Johnny Appleseed, and said, "Yes, he too made American history."